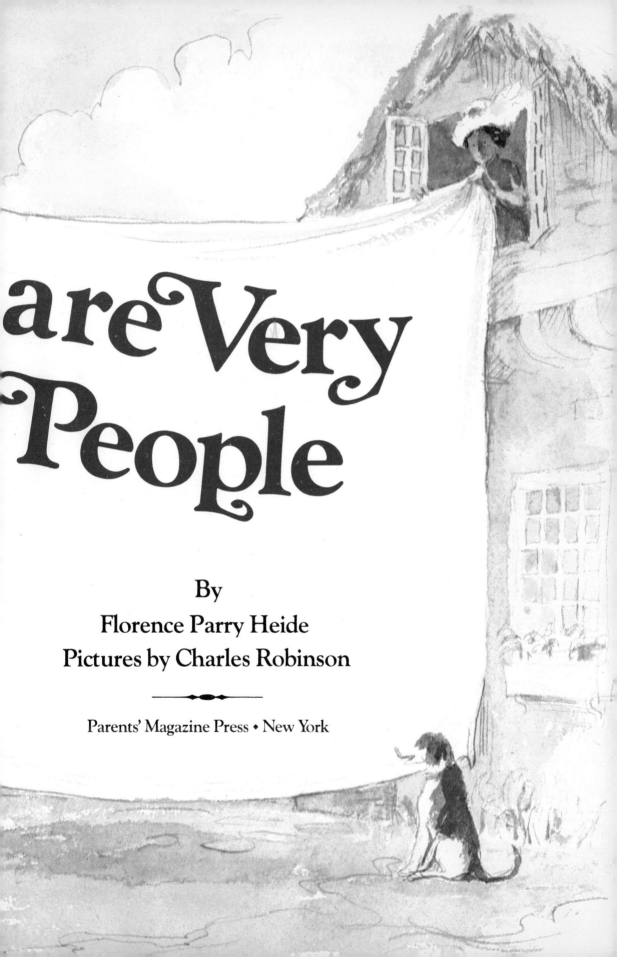

are Very
People

By
Florence Parry Heide
Pictures by Charles Robinson

—◆—

Parents' Magazine Press • New York

For my daughter Roxanne (otherwise known as Roxy) with much love

Everybody's afraid of something.

But Bigelow was afraid of EVERYTHING.

Well, not everything. He wasn't afraid of his mother, for instance. But he was afraid of just about everything else.

He was afraid of clouds.

"They might fall on me," he said.

He was afraid of alphabet soup.

"What if I swallowed letters that spelled a magic word that would turn me into a mushroom?" he asked.

He was afraid of the rain, so he carried a big red umbrella everywhere, even on the sunniest days.

"Rain might melt me," said Bigelow.

"Nonsense," said his mother. "Why would rain melt you? It's just water. You don't melt in the bathtub, dear, and *that's* water."

As soon as she'd said it she was sorry, because then Bigelow wouldn't take a bath — not without a lot of fuss, anyway.

"You needn't wear your raincoat in the tub, dear," said his mother.

One day Bigelow was out walking. It was bathtime,
and he thought he'd rather walk outside and take a chance
on the clouds falling on him. If he saw one coming,
he could jump away. It was better than melting
in the bathtub, certainly.

He was so busy looking up at the clouds that he didn't
look where he was going. And the first thing he knew
he heard someone doing a lot of very shrill screaming.

He looked down and saw a little lady running around
on the ground. Bigelow had never seen such a little lady.

"Excuse me," said Bigelow, "is that you screaming down
there? Is there anything wrong?"

"Wrong?" cried the little lady. "What's wrong is that you're stepping on my garden, and the next thing I know you'll be stepping on *me*."

"Of course I won't step on you," said Bigelow. "I was just looking up in the air, checking the clouds, instead of down at my feet, checking the chances of stepping on very small people. Now that I know you're down there, I'll be very careful."

"Go away, go away!" screamed the lady. "I'm afraid you might eat me up!"

"Eat you?" asked Bigelow. "Why would I eat you?"

"Because you're a giant, that's why!"

"I am?" asked Bigelow in surprise. "I didn't think I was a giant. I just thought you were very small."

The lady peered up at Bigelow.

"You didn't know you were a giant?" she asked.

"Of course not. Everyone I know is my size. Regular size, that is," said Bigelow. "I never saw a little wee person like you before."

"I'm regular size," said the lady, whose name
was Mrs. Pimberly. Mrs. Peter Pimberly.

"Oh, no," said Bigelow politely, "*I'm* regular size,
I'm sure. You are just extremely small."

He started to sit down.

"Not on my house!" screamed Mrs. Pimberly.

Bigelow found a place that was not the house,
or the garden, or Mrs. Pimberly, and sat down.

Mrs. Pimberly came closer.

"I thought giants were very fierce," said Mrs. Pimberly.

"Well, they are, I believe," said Bigelow. "Being just regular size, I am not particularly fierce myself. In fact, I'm afraid of just about everything."

"You are?" asked Mrs. Pimberly.

"Yes, I'm afraid so," said Bigelow unhappily.

"In all the books I've read, giants are very fierce," insisted Mrs. Pimberly. "I never travel, so I've never seen any before today. But I'm sure they're fierce if the books say so."

Now that she had stopped screaming, Mrs. Pimberly was speaking very softly, and Bigelow leaned closer to hear her. She screamed again and jumped away.

"I just wanted to hear you better," said Bigelow. "Would you mind if I put you on my shoulder? Then I wouldn't have to listen so hard."

Mrs. Pimberly looked up. "It's not a trick, is it?" she asked. "You won't get me up there and *then* eat me?"

"Of course not," said Bigelow. He picked her up and put her on his shoulder.

"It wouldn't matter, your being afraid of things," said Mrs. Pimberly, "except that you're a giant, and giants are very brave people."

Bigelow decided not to argue any more about the giant business. After all, if she realized she was really so small, it might make her nervous, and she was nervous enough already.

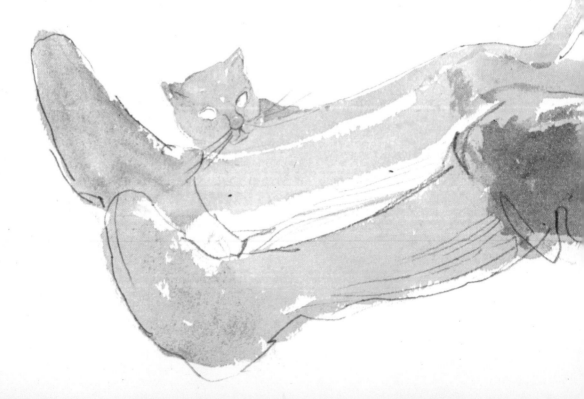

"It matters to me that I'm afraid," said Bigelow sadly.
"I mean, it's boring. Like right now, I'm afraid that
when I stand up I might hit my head on the sky."

"That's silly," said Mrs. Pimberly positively.

"It's easy for you to say it's silly," said Bigelow,
"when you're never going to bump *your* head on the sky.
Unless, of course, you're still on my shoulder when
I stand up. Then you might."

"Nonsense," said Mrs. Pimberly. "You know what I think?
I think that if you *acted* very brave, you'd *feel* very brave."

"You do?" asked Bigelow doubtfully.

"For instance," said Mrs. Pimberly, "if you would go
around shouting a giant sort of shout, that would make
you feel braver."

"What's a giant sort of shout?" asked Bigelow.

"Well, the only one I can think of offhand is *Fee Fi Fo Fum*,"
said Mrs. Pimberly. "All giants know that one.
I'm surprised your mother hasn't taught it to you yet.
Why don't you practice it for a while, and I'll go in
and make some tea."

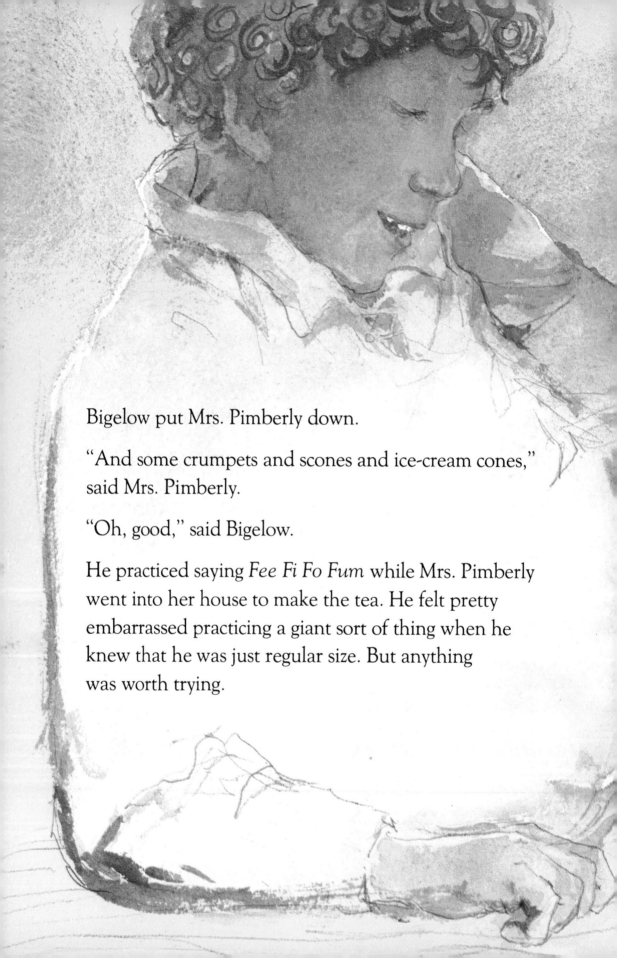

Bigelow put Mrs. Pimberly down.

"And some crumpets and scones and ice-cream cones," said Mrs. Pimberly.

"Oh, good," said Bigelow.

He practiced saying *Fee Fi Fo Fum* while Mrs. Pimberly went into her house to make the tea. He felt pretty embarrassed practicing a giant sort of thing when he knew that he was just regular size. But anything was worth trying.

He was just saying *Fee Fi Fo Fum* very softly to himself
for the eighty-seventh time when Mrs. Pimberly
came out with the tea things.

"*FEE FI FO FUM*," said Bigelow in a loud voice.

Mrs. Pimberly threw up her arms and screamed.
Then she saw Bigelow sitting there.

"Goodness gracious sakes alive," said Mrs. Pimberly.
"You certainly scared me. That's a very good shout.
I'm sure it will make you feel much, much braver."

She looked at the ground. "I spilled all the tea things,"
she said, and went into her house to get a broom
and dustpan.

"It was all my fault," said Bigelow, as Mrs. Pimberly
swept up the crumbs and the broken dishes.
"I'm sorry I frightened you and made you break your dishes
and spill the tea. And the crumpets and scones
and ice-cream cones," he added wistfully.

"It was only my second-best tea set, really," said Mrs. Pimberly. "But I'm afraid that's the last of the crumpets and scones and ice-cream cones. I hope you're not hungry."

"I'm starved," confessed Bigelow. "I could eat *anything*."

"You could?" Mrs. Pimberly moved uneasily toward the door of her house.

"Not you, of course," said Bigelow hastily. "But just about anything else."

"Would you like some nice alphabet soup?" asked Mrs. Pimberly.

"No, thank you," said Bigelow. "I'm afraid that I'm afraid of alphabet soup. I'm not afraid of pancakes, though," he added.

So Mrs. Pimberly went in to make some pancakes. Bigelow carefully turned over and lay on his stomach. He propped himself up on his elbows so he could see in the kitchen window.

Mrs. Pimberly made pancakes. Lots of pancakes. As fast as she made them, she handed them through the window.

"There now," she said after a while. "That's the last of the pancakes."

Bigelow's face fell. The pancakes were so tiny they had hardly been a mouthful. He'd better go home to a regular-size meal, he thought.

"I don't know how your mother manages to feed you," said Mrs. Pimberly, coming outside. "That was seventy-three pancakes."

"My mother's pancakes are pretty big," explained Bigelow.

"*Mine* were pretty big," said Mrs. Pimberly.

"Yes, of course," said Bigelow politely. "And very delicious. And thank you very much. For the pancakes, and for the *Fee Fi Fo Fum* thing. I'm sure it will help me in getting braver."

Bigelow stood up. He ducked a little, in case he was going to hit his head on the sky. But he didn't, and that made him feel a little braver. Not much, but a little.

The sun was bright and Bigelow saw his shadow on the ground.

Usually, Bigelow was afraid of his shadow. Now he said, "*Fee Fi Fo Fum.*"

The shadow still looked pretty scary, so Bigelow stopped looking at it altogether.

He looked up to see where the clouds were. There weren't any. Good, thought Bigelow. It was a little too soon to practice being brave about the clouds.

"Would you like to come home with me?" asked Bigelow politely. "I'd like my parents to meet you. Otherwise they won't believe me."

"What size are your parents?" asked Mrs. Pimberly cautiously.

"Regular parent size," said Bigelow.

"Just as I thought," said Mrs. Pimberly. "Bigger than you.
I think," said Mrs. Pimberly, "I *think* it would be best
if you visited me, instead of the other way around.
And actually," she said, not wanting to hurt his feelings,
"actually I never visit anyone of *any* size. I never go
anywhere. I never travel or anything."

Mrs. Pimberly sighed. "I've never even been on a train,"
she said wistfully. "That's probably why I've never seen
any giants before. You have to travel to see things like
giants."

"I'd be afraid to travel," said Bigelow to himself. "I might
see a giant." Aloud he said, "I'll go on home for supper,
if that's all right with you."

"Oh, *quite* all right," Mrs. Pimberly assured him.
"Do try to come back tomorrow to practice being brave.
Come *after* you've eaten," she added.

Bigelow said good-bye and started home.

Supper was ready, and it was alphabet soup again.

"*Fee Fi Fo Fum*," said Bigelow.

"What, dear?" asked his mother.

Bigelow looked at the soup. What if he *did* swallow letters that spelled a magic word that would turn him into a mushroom? He'd never forgive himself.

"*Fee Fi Fo Fum*," he said again, louder, and started to eat the soup. He ate it all. All but the letters. He left them, just to be on the safe side. He'd eaten the *soup* part, anyway. Mrs. Pimberly would be very proud, he thought.

Since he hadn't had his bath at the usual bathtime, it was bathtime now. It was always bathtime, thought Bigelow.

"*Fee Fi Fo Fum*," said Bigelow.

"What, dear?" asked his mother.

Bigelow sighed and climbed into the tub.

"Are we giants?" asked Bigelow while he was having his bath.

"Giants?" asked his mother. "Oh, no, dear. Giants are very big. We're just regular size."

"I met someone very small today," said Bigelow.
"*She* thought I was a giant."

"That's nice, dear. You're growing up to be a big boy,
that's probably what she meant."

"Oh," said Bigelow.

"*Fee Fi Fo Fum*," said Bigelow to himself as he climbed
out of the tub. Thank goodness he hadn't melted
that time.

Really, thought Bigelow, as he took off his rubbers
and raincoat and dried himself off, I do think I'm getting
a little braver, after all.

The next morning, after a breakfast of regular-size pancakes, he played with his train. He had a very nice train. It had an engine, and a freight car, and a passenger car, and a caboose.

A passenger car.

Bigelow thought for a moment. Then he got a big box. He packed each car very carefully in the box. He took the train track apart and packed *it* in the box. Then he carried the box downstairs and outside and walked until he came to Mrs. Pimberly's house.

He set the track up and he connected the cars of the train and then he knelt down to the kitchen window. He whispered, "Good morning, Mrs. Pimberly," very softly so as not to frighten her.

Mrs. Pimberly looked out. "Goodness gracious sakes alive!" said Mrs. Pimberly. "A real train!"

"All aboard!" called Bigelow, as he wound up the engine.

Mrs. Pimberly ran out of her house and climbed into the passenger car.

Away went the train and away went Mrs. Pimberly, round and round and round the track.

"I'm really traveling," said Mrs. Pimberly happily.
She ran out to the caboose and waved to Bigelow
each time the train came around to where he was sitting.
"You can see a lot when you travel," said Mrs. Pimberly.
"Giants and everything."

Bigelow was so busy waving to Mrs. Pimberly
that he forgot to be afraid of the clouds or his shadow.
He even forgot to say *Fee Fi Fo Fum*.

After all, giants are very brave people.